W9-BNU-215

To hat lovers everywhere
and the kids at
Waipahu Elementary School

DON'T TOUCH MY HAT!

James Rumford

Alfred A. Knopf New York

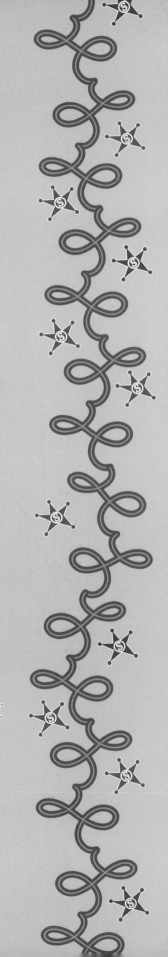

LAKE COUNTY PUBLIC LIBRARY

Out West, a lonesome prairie or two from anywhere, was a town called Sunshine.

Sunshine was smaller'n most,
bigger'n some, but cleaner and
more civ'lized than 'em all.
Sheriff John saw to that—
him and his ten-gallon hat.

Why, with that hat on, he could round up rustlers, stop saloon fights, and deliver ladies in distress.

Bank robbers, train robbers, stagecoach robbers,
any kinda robbers didn't have a chance 'gainst
Sheriff John and his ten-gallon hat.

Without that sweat-stiff, trail-dusted, bullet-riddled hat, Sheriff John could do nothing—or so he thought.

So, when he was at the barber's, it was:

"FELLERS, DON'T TOUCH MY HAT!"

Takin' his Saturday bath:

"SUGAR,
DON'T TOUCH
MY HAT!"

Afore he turned out the light:

"NOW, DARLIN', DON'T TOUCH MY HAT!"

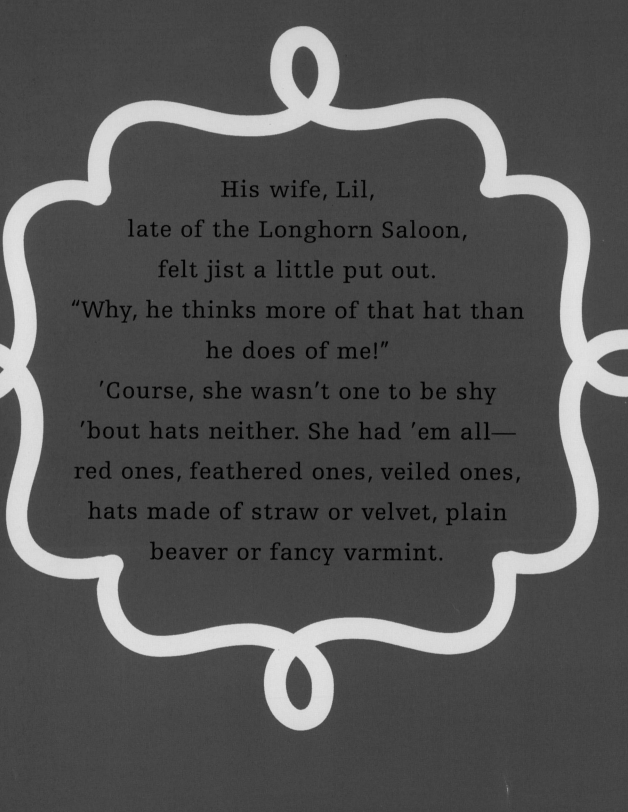

His wife, Lil,
late of the Longhorn Saloon,
felt jist a little put out.
"Why, he thinks more of that hat than
he does of me!"
'Course, she wasn't one to be shy
'bout hats neither. She had 'em all—
red ones, feathered ones, veiled ones,
hats made of straw or velvet, plain
beaver or fancy varmint.

And yesterday, to top it all,
she came a-prancin' home
with the fanciest one yet.

And so, on a quiet western night—moonless
and coyote-less—Sheriff John and Lil had
just turned down the light when . . .
the Ol' West went completely wild!

Rustlers were at
McDermott's ranch, robbers in
the bank. There was a fight at the saloon
and a range war a-brewin'.

"Sheriff!" yelled Deputy Bob. "Sheriff!
Come quick! There's trouble aplenty!"

No time for lantern lightin'. Sheriff
John pulled on his pants, jumped into
his boots, strapped on his gun. . . .

"I'm a-comin', Bob.
JIST LET ME
GIT MY HAT!"

"Darlin' sugar!" wailed Lil,
half hangin' out of the upstairs
window. But it was too late.
Sheriff John and Deputy Bob
were long gone.

Sheriff John put a stop to the fight.

He caught the robbers at the safe,

rounded up the rustlers,

and made peace
betwixt the sheep herders
and the cattlemen.

All before sunup,
thanks to his trusty ten-gallon hat.
But when he got back home,
Lil was a-waitin' for him. Let's just say
that Sheriff John had a lot of rethinkin'
to do, best summed up by this:

IT'S YOUR HEART,
NOT YOUR HAT.

"Sorry, darlin', I ruint your new hat."

"Sugar, I'm jist glad you're home safe and sound."

THE END